forevermore
love
ALEX
USA TODAY BESTSELLING AUTHOR
GRAYSON

Forevermore

Cover Design by Moonstruck Cover Design. Interior Formatting by Alex Grayson. Editing by Edits by Erin and Briggs Consulting LLC.

ISBN: 978-1-7351982-3-1 (Paperback)

ISBN: 978-1-7351982-4-8 (Hardback)

ISBN: 978-1-7351982-1-7 (Ebook)

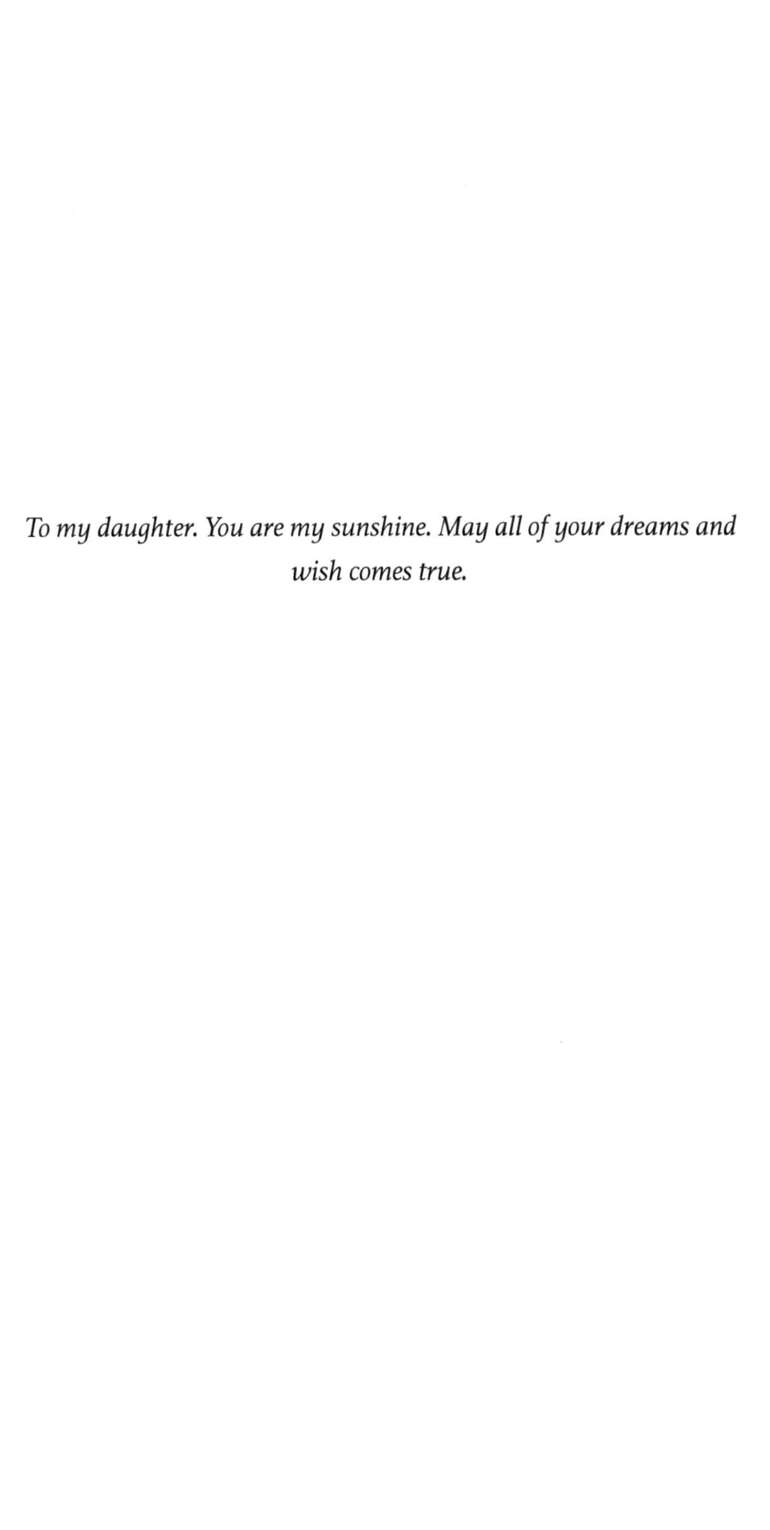

To my daughter. You are my sunshine. May all of your dreams and wish comes true.

CHAPTER ONE

MOLLY
Barre Vale, New York
7 Years Old

"Four-eyes! Four-eyes! Four-eyes!"

My bottom lip trembles, and hot tears slide down my cheeks as Mark and Jensen tease me. I wish I remembered to take my glasses off before coming out to recess. I don't know why they hate me so much, but they always pick on me. This time it's because of the stupid glasses Mom is making me wear. I wish they'd leave me alone.

I cross my arms over my chest, turn around, and sulk over to the swing set, trying my best to ignore their taunts. My shoulders droop when I hear them following me. Keeping my head down, I sit on the swing.

"Four—"

"Leave her alone!"

I jerk my head up at the angry voice. My breath catches at the black-haired boy with his back to me, blocking Mark and Jensen. It's the new kid from my class who just started today. Mrs. Garner said his name is Lincoln. I wonder if he's stupid or very brave because no one ever stands up to these two bullies.

"What are you gonna do if we don't?" Jensen taunts. He puffs his chest out like he's trying to act bigger than he is. If it wouldn't cause more problems for me, I'd probably laugh.

"You're gonna find out if you don't leave her alone," Lincoln says, taking a step closer to him.

Something happens that I never thought I'd see. With Lincoln's back to me, I can't see his face. His expression must be scary though, because Jensen drops his eyes and takes a step back. Mark's face turns white, and he trips over his feet trying to get away and almost falls on his butt. I kinda wish he would have.

My belly stops tumbling when Jensen and Mark turn and run to the slide, looking back over their shoulders as they go.

"Thank you," I mumble. I sway back and forth on the swing, the tips of my toes grazing the wood chips covering the ground.

When Lincoln turns to face me, the look on his face scares me at first, but it doesn't last long. As soon as his eyes meet mine, the mean look is gone. He has the prettiest eyes I've ever seen. They remind me of the sky when there's a storm coming. His black hair is long and messy on the top but cut shorter on the sides.

"Do they do that a lot?" he asks, pushing his hands into his front pockets.

I've only ever told one person about Mark and Jensen picking on me. I went to my teacher last year, and she called all of our parents in for a conference. The talk she gave them didn't do any good. It made their behavior even worse. A week later, they pushed me down on the playground, and I scraped my knee and palm on the woodchips. They normally don't touch me, but their words hurt more anyway. I haven't told anyone since then, worried about what they'll do if I did.

For some reason though, I want to tell Lincoln.

"Not all the time." I shrug.

"Well, they won't anymore when I'm around. I'll protect you."

Something weird happens inside my stomach. It feels like there's a bunch of butterflies flying around.

I stare at him as he walks over to the swing beside me. Mom would say it's rude to stare, but I don't care. It's like something is making me look at him. I don't think I could stop even if I wanted to.

"What's your name?" he asks after he sits down and starts pushing his swing with his foot.

"Molly."

When he looks at me, I jerk my head forward, my cheeks turning hot at being caught watching him.

"I like it."

I peek at him again. "What do you mean?"

"Your name. I like it. It's pretty."

"Oh." A smile pops up on my face. "Thanks."

As we continue to swing, my eyes keep going back to him. I *really* like looking at him.

My glasses slip down my nose, so I push them back. I've thought about purposely dropping them and stomping on them, but I don't want Mom to be disappointed in me. She stressed the importance of taking care of them.

"Thank you for making Jensen and Mark stop."

He lifts his shoulders. "They're jerks."

I nod. "Yeah. I don't know why they don't like me. I haven't ever done anything to them."

"It's because they think you're pretty," he grumbles.

My eyes widen. "What? No, they don't."

He looks at me out the corner of his eye. "Mom says boys pick on girls because they think they're pretty."

I pinch my lips together. I want to tell him that's dumb, but I don't want him to think I'm saying his mom is dumb. Another thought occurs to me. If his mom is right, then does that mean he doesn't think I'm pretty since he's not making fun of me? My shoulders slump with the thought. I want him to think I'm pretty, just like he thinks my name is.

We don't talk anymore as we swing until the bell rings. Lincoln jumps up and surprises me when he waits for me to stand too. He walks beside me as we make our way over to Mrs. Garner, our teacher. When Jensen and Mark get close, Lincoln gives them a dirty look and they move away.

"So, do you wanna be friends?"

He looks at me, smiling so big his cheeks puff out. "We already are."

I smile too, suddenly feeling really happy.

WITH MY BOOK bag on my back and my lunch box in my hand, I climb the bus steps. I always sit in the front seat right behind the bus driver, Mrs. Willis, so I'm surprised when someone is already there. Lincoln looks just as surprised as I am. He quickly gets up and moves to the aisle.

"Cool," he says, grinning. "We can sit together."

The butterflies are back in my belly as I slide into the seat with my lunch box on my lap. Lincoln sits beside me, and I notice his lunch box.

"I like your lunch box."

He glances down at it before looking back at me. "Thanks. I painted the front."

"Wow! Really?" I scoot over and take a closer look. It doesn't have any pictures or anything. It's only a bunch of colorful squiggly lines and splashes, like he dipped his paintbrush in a bunch of different colors and flicked it at the box. It looks really neat. "That's so cool. It's a lot better than mine."

He looks at my pink Hello Kitty lunch box. "I can paint yours, too, if you want."

"But mine already has a picture on it."

"All I gotta do is paint it white first, then do whatever design I want."

I drop my eyes to the pink lunch box and wonder if Mom would be mad if I let Lincoln paint it. I decide to take the chance and hand it over to him.

"Here, you can use mine until I get done with yours." He hands over his lunch box. "It'll take me a few days to finish it."

"But what will you use for your lunch?"

"I've got another one at home."

"Okay." I hug the lunch box to my chest. It's dumb, but I like the thought of using something that's his.

Mrs. Willis pulls away from the school, causing our shoulders to bump together.

"You like to paint, huh?"

He nods. "Yep. It's my favorite thing to do. Mom says I'm going to be an artist when I grow up, just like Dad."

"Your dad paints too?"

"Nah. He likes to draw with pencils, not paint like me."

"I suck at drawing and painting."

"You could totally get better. You just havta put your mind to it."

"Maybe you could teach me how?"

I hold my breath, hoping he'll agree. It'll mean I get to spend more time with him.

"Sure. I can show you."

The bus stops and a couple of kids get off. There's only one more stop left before we reach mine.

"Where did you live before?"

"West Virginia."

I tilt my head to see him better. "Why did you move here?"

He shrugs, "Something to do with my dad's job. He's supposed to get paid a lot more or something."

"Oh." I look at the back of Mrs. Willis' head for a moment before turning back to Lincoln. "Do you miss your old home and friends?"

He presses his lips together, like he's thinking hard about something. "I did, but not anymore."

"Whatcha mean?"

Before he can answer, the bus stops again, and more kids get off. My stop isn't far from here. It's Friday, so there's no school tomorrow, which means it'll be two whole days before I see Lincoln again. The thought of not seeing him for that long makes my stomach hurt like it does when I eat too much candy.

"'Cause I made a new friend that I like a lot."

My cheeks feel hot, knowing he's talking about me.

"My birthday is in a couple of weeks. Do you wanna come to my party?"

His smile is so big it takes up almost his whole face. He bobs his head up and down. "Yeah. That sounds like fun. My birthday was a week ago. I wish we had been friends then so you could have come to mine."

"I can come to the next one," I offer.

"You gotta come. People never miss their best friend's parties."

I can't help the smile that forms on my face. "You wanna be my best friend?"

He looks at me like I'm crazy or something. "We're already best friends."

My smile grows, but it soon fades when the bus starts to slow down. My shoulders drop, and my stomach hurts again.

"What's wrong?" He frowns.

"This is my stop, but I don't wanna get off," I mumble.

"Why not?"

I drop my head a little, feeling shy. My hair falls across my face, but I still peek at him through the red strands. "'Cause I like talking to you, and I'm not going to be able to see you for two whole days."

My eyes go as big as saucers when he pushes it back from my face and over my shoulder.

"I like talking to you too. You're really nice and super pretty."

His words make that weird fluttering feeling come back to my stomach.

"Guess what?" Lincoln asks when the bus stops and he gets up to let me out of the seat.

"What?"

"This is my stop too." He grins and his pretty eyes dance with laughter.

"Really?" I stare at him in shock. "You're really for real?"

He grabs his backpack from the floor. "Yep."

Excitement bubbles inside me and almost has me tripping in the aisle. When I tip forward, he grabs my arm and keeps me from falling. It's stupid, but I can't help the giddiness I feel, knowing he's getting off at my stop. Maybe that means he doesn't live far from me and we can play over the weekend.

I wave goodbye to Mrs. Willis when I walk past her, and she wishes us both a good weekend. It definitely looks better than it did before.

"Which way is your house?" Lincoln asks once the bus pulls away.

I point down the street. "It's that way."

"Well, let's go then."

He grabs my hand and we start walking. He doesn't let it go, and I'm glad. I like his hand touching mine. It makes me feel special.

When we come to the corner where I have to turn right, I expect him to let go of my hand. He keeps a hold of it, and we both turn down my street.

"Your house is this way too?"

"Yep." He points to a big white house down the road.

"No way!" I exclaim. "That's my house right there!" I point to the light blue house only a couple away from his.

"Awesome!" His fingers twitch against mine. "That means we can play all the time."

My cheeks hurt from smiling so much. I'm going to have a real friend, and he lives really close to me. There's only one other girl who lives on this street, and she's a couple of years older than me. Her parents take her to school every morning and pick her up in the afternoon. The other girls in my class aren't very nice, so I never tried making friends with them.

"Maybe you can come over to my house tomorrow?" he suggests.

We come to a stop in front of my house, and he lets my hand go. "I can ask my mom. She'll probably want to meet your parents first, though. I've never played at someone else's house before, except for my cousins."

"I'll ask Mom to come over, so your mom knows you'll be okay."

I nod, wishing it was tomorrow already. "I gotta go inside before she comes looking for me."

"Okay." His pretty eyes crinkle at the sides when he smiles. "I'll see you tomorrow."

"Bye, Lincoln," I say softly.

"Bye, Molly."

I'm sad when I turn around and walk up the driveway, but hopefully, I'll get to see him tomorrow. I look back when I get to my front door and see him still standing on the sidewalk, watching me. I smile and wave before I open the door and walk inside.

CHAPTER TWO

LINCOLN
8 Years Old

Staring up at the big, white door with a black knocker thing, I press the doorbell instead. I bounce in my shoes as I wait for it to open. Excitement has my heart jumping around in my chest, like it always does when I'm about to see Molly.

The door opens, and I expect to see her mom or dad on the other side, so I'm surprised and happy when Molly peeks her head around the door. All I can do is stare at her. She has on a light-blue dress with little purple flowers at the bottom where it touches her knees. Her pretty, red hair is braided and tossed over her shoulder, and her green eyes, which always remind me of the color of grass after it rains, sparkle like she has little fireflies in them.

"Hey." I smile and wave.

Cute dimples pop out on her cheeks when she smiles back. She pushes her glasses up her little nose. "You came."

"Told you I would. Best friends always come to their best friend's birthday parties. I won't ever miss any of yours." I hold out her wrapped gift. "This is for you."

Her eyes dart to the present in my hand and widen like she's surprised. "You got me a birthday present?"

"Of course I did, silly. What kind of friend would I be if I didn't?"

She giggles and grabs the present, hugging it to her chest. "Thank you."

"Happy Birthday, Molly."

She reaches for my hand, and the minute she touches it, some weird feeling travels up my arm. Her skin is warm and soft as I curl my fingers around hers.

"Come on. Everyone's out back."

With my hand still in hers, she leads me through her house toward the back door. I've been here a few times in the two weeks we've known each other, just like she's been to my house. Almost every day since we met on the playground, we've hung out together.

At first, I was angry we moved here because I had to leave all my friends and my favorite after school art program. I refused to go to school the first day, but Mom and Dad made me. I hated them so much when they left me at the classroom door to walk inside. I didn't care I had to go in alone, I just didn't want to be there. I had just sat at my desk, angrily pulling out my pencil box, when I looked up and saw the prettiest girl in the whole world come into the room. She had her head bent down, looking at something in her hand, so her red hair was hiding her face, but I knew I had to know her. Something inside my head told me we were going to be friends.

I didn't get a chance to talk to her until we went out for recess. Mrs. Garner kept me inside for the first few minutes to talk, but as soon as I walked through the doors, I immediately looked for her. I saw her with a couple of other boys. I didn't care. I was going to go over there and steal her attention away from them.

I was on my way when I heard them call her "four-eyes." They started laughing, and she turned away from them, dropping her head and shoulders. It made me so mad I ran the rest of the way. I wanted to punch their ugly faces for making her sad. Instead, I made them leave, sat beside her on the other swing, and we talked until she smiled. The pain in my chest didn't ease up until then.

It's weird because it seems like ever since I met her, my chest hurts when I'm not with her. Even now, that pain didn't go away until she opened the door and I saw her pretty face.

She smiles at me as she pulls open the back door. Keeping my hand in hers, we walk out back into the hot air. There are a bunch of people all over the backyard. Most of them are adults, but there are a few other kids I don't know. She pulls me to one of the picnic tables and lets go of my hand. After arranging my present, so it sits perfectly straight against one of the bigger gifts, she turns around.

"Did you paint the paper?"

"Yep," I answer. She liked the picture I painted on her lunch box, and I hope she likes the one I painted on the wrapping paper.

"I really like it. I'm gonna keep the paper when I open it."

Her words make my stomach flip.

"Molly! Come play hide and seek with us!"

She looks over at whoever hollered, but I keep my eyes on her. I don't know why, but I like looking at her.

"That's my cousin, Bryanne. You wanna come play hide and seek with us?"

I'd do anything she wants to do. "Yeah."

With a grin, she grabs my hand and we run over to the small group of kids. We play rock, paper, scissors to find out who's going to be the seeker. My paper loses to Molly's scissors. I count to fifty while everyone else hides. Spinning around, I dart my eyes all over the backyard. I spot someone almost right away, and with a smirk, I head straight for the picnic table with food on it. I get to my knees and look underneath. Troy, another one of Molly's younger cousins, looks at me with wide eyes.

"Gotcha!"

His shoulders hunch when I touch his ankle. "Ahh man... I always get found first."

I laugh before turning to start hunting again.

I find two more kids; neither of them the person I really want to find. I walk around the yard, looking under the other tables, behind trees, and any other hiding spots I come across, but still can't find Molly.

Hearing snickers, I turn and see Bryanne watching me. She has her hand over her mouth, like she's covering up a laugh.

"She's the best hider. I bet you'll never guess where she is."

"I will," I huff and turn back around. She can't hide forever. I'll find her. I always will.

We're supposed to stay in the backyard where the adults can see us, but I sneak around the corner of the house in case Molly didn't follow the rules. Of course, Molly's a good girl, so I should have known she wouldn't break the rules.

I come back around to the backyard when I notice something red flash in one of the trees. Narrowing my eyes, I keep watching the spot and run over to the tree. It's big with a lot of green leaves and thick branches. Once I'm underneath the low branches, I look up. Molly is above me, halfway up the tree sitting on a limb, smiling down at me. I grin back at her.

"Found ya."

She giggles. "Took you long enough. I thought I was going to be up here allll day."

I tilt my head. "Well, you could've told me you're the master at hiding."

"It was more fun watching you look for me."

I laugh, but it quickly dies away when she tucks her dress between her knees, grabs a branch, and swings her feet out from under her. I hold my breath until her feet land on another branch below her. She does this over and over again. I swear my heart has moved to my ears because the pounding in them is so loud. I don't breathe until she's standing in front of me, her smiling eyes locked on mine.

"What's wrong?" she asks, noticing my panicked expression.

"I was scared you'd fall."

My world would end if something happened to Molly. She's only been my best friend for two weeks, but I feel like I've known her my whole life.

"S'okay. I'm a really good tree climber too. Just ask anyone here. They'll tell you."

I shake my head. "Don't matter how good you are. You could still slip and fall. And anyway, I'll always worry about my girl. Forever."

A smile stretches across her face. "Forever?"

"Forevermore."

"You promise?"

I smile back and give her a promise I'll never ever break. "I promise."

"Molly!" her mom hollers. "It's time to open presents!"

"Yah!"

She grabs my hand and pulls me across the yard. I laugh because I'm happy. Happier than I've ever been before. And it's all because of Molly.

She tugs me beside her when she reaches the table filled with presents, telling me to sit right next to her. I don't argue. I'll always be where she wants me to be, no matter what I have to do to get there.

She starts ripping open presents, her grin getting bigger and bigger. After opening each one, she thanks the giver and gives them a hug. She saves mine for last. I don't know why, but I really like that. It's like she's saving the best for last. I'm both nervous and anxious to see what she thinks.

She's careful when she pulls the paper away, treating it like it's something precious, as if she really plans to keep it like she said she would. Her eyes grow big as she runs her fingers gently over the picture in front of her. It's a light purple and blue sky full of twinkling fireflies. The fireflies remind me of her eyes.

"This is so pretty, Lincoln," she breathes, still mesmerized. I feel like my chest is expanding to twice its size. I'm so happy she likes it.

She flips open the cover to the first blank page, and I step closer to look down at it with her. "It's a journal. I don't know if you have one yet, but I figured if you did, you could use this one when yours is full."

Lifting her head, her twinkling eyes meet mine. I know what happiness looks like, but I honestly can't say I've ever seen someone look so pleased before.

"I love it." Her dimples pop out again. "I don't have a journal, but I'll definitely use this one. I'm going to use it for all of our adventures together. It'll be a book about only you and me."

I really like the sound of that, because I know we'll share a lot of adventures. I hated my parents for moving me here, but now I know this is where I'm meant to be. I was supposed to meet Molly, and we're supposed to be best friends forever.

Forever and more.

CHAPTER THREE

LINCOLN

11 Years Old

We both lie on our backs staring up at the dark sky filled with twinkling stars. I have my hands folded under my head, and Molly lies with her hands laced together on her stomach. The grass is damp beneath us from the dew, but we don't care.

It's late, so late, both of our parents would have a fit if they knew we were out here. I haven't been able to see Molly the last couple of days because they had to go out of town for her grandfather's funeral. I wanted to go with them to be there for Molly, but my parents wouldn't let me, saying it was a time for family only. They don't get it. I am Molly's family. Or part of it, anyway.

I was utterly miserable while she was gone. I missed her like crazy, but I also worried she was sad. A sad Molly makes my chest ache.

I knew they were coming back today, but it was too late for me to go over. There was no way I was going to wait until tomorrow to see her, so I waited until my parents went to bed and snuck out through my window. All of the lights were off at Molly's, so I knew her parents were in bed too. Molly was wide awake and waiting for me when I tapped on her window. She knew I wasn't going to wait until tomorrow, either. As soon as I was through the window, we hugged like we hadn't seen each other in months. It wasn't until that moment that the pain in my chest faded.

"Holy smokes," she says excitedly, pointing up to the sky. "Did you see that one, Lincoln?"

I didn't, because I was too busy looking at Molly.

"Was it a big one?" I ask, looking to where she's pointing.

"It was huge! It streaked all the way across the sky."

Tonight isn't the first night we've lain in the grass looking for falling stars—we've done it a bunch of times—but it is the first night I haven't paid much attention to the sky. I've looked at Molly more than I have anything else. I have a lot to make up for from not seeing her for two whole days.

"Did you make a wish?"

"Yep," she chirps. I don't have to look to know she's smiling. "The next one, you get to make a wish."

I already know what my wish will be. It's the same one I wish for every time.

“Look!” She sits up suddenly, and I do the same. “It’s a firefly.”

“I thought they only came out right after the sun goes down.”

She gets to her knees and holds out her hand, waiting to see if it’ll land on her palm. “Maybe she’s lost,” she suggests.

“It’s a he,” I inform her.

She glances at me over her shoulder. “How do you know?”

I watch as the firefly hovers over her palm for several seconds, its butt flashing a couple of times before landing on the tip of her finger.

“Because it’s the boy who flies, looking for a girl. They flash their butts and wait for a girl to flash back at them. If they like the flashes, they mate.”

“Mate?”

I grin and whisper, “They have babies.”

She gives me a weird look and wrinkles her nose. “That’s gross. I heard an eighth-grader talking about....” She stops and drops her head down, her hair falling forward so I can’t see her face.

I tuck it back behind her ear. I can see her face now, but she keeps her eyes darted away. “Talking about what?”

After a moment, she leans forward and lowers her voice. “She said to make babies, you have to have sex.”

I almost laugh at the horrified look on her face. We’re only eleven and probably not supposed to know about sex, but we’re in middle school, and the older kids talk. While the idea of sex sounds messy and disgusting, it also seems—interesting. I’d never tell Molly that, though. She'd probably throw something at me and call me a weirdo.

"Yeah, but if they don't do that, then the boy fireflies will always just fly around. Don't you want them to be happy?"

She thinks for a minute, looking back at the firefly still on her finger. "I guess." She grins. "I'll just think of it like they're looking for their best friend and forget about the icky part." Her grin turns into a frown. "I hope he's not lost, and he finds her."

God, but I missed her so much. I never want to go another day without seeing her. If she ever has to leave town again, I'll sneak inside their trunk. Mom will kill me later when I get home, but it'll be worth it.

"How do you know that stuff about fireflies?" She twists her hand from side to side, looking at the little beetle.

I shrug and lean back on my hands. "I found a book in the library about them."

"I didn't know you liked them so much."

The only reason I do is because of her eyes. They remind me of fireflies when their butts flash. The brilliant-green light perfectly matches the color of her eyes.

The firefly leaves her finger, and his butt immediately starts blinking. We both watch as it slowly flies away. There's a small flash of light on the short grass not far from us.

"Looks like he found his mate," I remark.

"His best friend," she corrects me with a smirk.

We lie back down, and this time I make sure to keep my eyes on the sky, not wanting to miss another shooting star and my chance at making a wish. It takes a while, but one streaks across the dark sky, leaving a white line trailing behind.

"It's your turn to make a wish."

And I do.

I wish that Molly will always be in my life, no matter what.

CHAPTER FOUR

MOLLY
13 Years Old

I huddle against the headboard with my knees pulled tight to my chest and my arms wrapped around my legs. I'm shaking so hard my teeth are chattering as I stare at the window. At the first flash of light, I squeeze my eyes shut, toss the blanket over my head, and slam my palms over my ears. Even through my hands, I hear the deep growly rumble of thunder.

I've always been scared of thunderstorms. They make me think of bad people stomping down the hallway as they come for me. It's dumb because nothing like that has ever happened before. Mom and Dad are the nicest people I know. They'd never hurt a fly, unless that fly was going to hurt me.

I hear the whoosh of the window opening, and I jerk my head from underneath the blanket. A head full of wet, jet-black hair appears first, followed by a lanky form. Forgetting about the storm for the moment, I toss the blanket aside, jump from my bed, and rush over to Lincoln.

"What are you doing?" I hiss, then dart my eyes to my bedroom door, worried my parents will come barging in at any moment. They love Lincoln, but I don't think they'd love him sneaking into my room after midnight. Dad caught him doing it once. He marched him right out of my room and straight into his office. Lincoln later told me he got a stern talking to. Dad told him if he needed to see me so bad that he had to sneak in through my window, he should just knock on the front door, and he would be let in. No matter the time. Lincoln still sneaks in, but not as often. If I'm honest, I'm glad he still does it because it makes me feel special.

Just not tonight. Tonight, I'm angry at him.

He stands to his full height, which at thirteen, is almost a foot taller than me, and shakes his shaggy hair. Water sprays me all over the face.

"I'm getting out of the rain. Don't you know it's pouring outside?"

I glare at the smile he gives me. It's the one he reserves only for me, and almost always makes me smile in return. It doesn't tonight though. I'm still mad at him for what happened earlier today. I'm also furious he put himself in danger.

"Are you stupid?" I ask, throwing my hands on my hips. He's so frustrating sometimes. "It's also storming outside, you dummy. The lightning and thunder are less than two seconds apart, which means the lightning is less than two miles away. You could have been struck."

"Nah." He shrugs. "I was safe." He turns toward me. It's dark in my room, but from the small lamp beside my bed, I can barely make out the gray in his eyes. The smile falls from his face. "Besides, I couldn't let my girl be alone during the storm."

And just like that, I get the same flutters in my stomach that I got the first day I met him, and have gotten hundreds of times since. He called me his girl for the first time on the day after we met, when he introduced me to his parents.

"Mom and Dad, this is my girl, Molly."

That day is one of my favorites. I have a lot of favorite days, they all have Lincoln in them. I remember the pure joy and warmth I felt when I heard him call me his girl. And each time since then, that warmth grows.

Which is why what he did earlier today hurt so much. I'm his girl, and it scares me to think of him having another one.

"And I am a dummy," he says quietly. I drag my eyes up from the floor and look at him. "I'm sorry about earlier."

My nose stings, and I shrug, hoping I don't start crying. "It's not your fault. It was stupid of me to get angry."

He steps closer, and my eyes lock on the drops of water sliding down his cheeks.

"You could never be stupid. You're one of the smartest people I know." He pushes back my hair that's fallen in my face. "But I swear it wasn't what it looked like."

I cross my arms over my chest and wait for him to continue.

"Sabastian asked me to sit with him for a few minutes so he could show me the new game on his Gameboy. He ended up getting sick and had to rush to the bathroom. I was about to get up when his sister sat down in his spot. She kept insisting she show me the game instead. I didn't want to—I swear I didn't—but I didn't want to be mean and ignore her."

This is the first year Lincoln and I don't have most of the same classes. The only period we share is lunch. I hate that I only get to see him for thirty minutes during school, so I really look forward to lunch. His class gets to the lunchroom a few minutes before mine, so he always saves a seat for me. Earlier today, when I saw him sitting with Bridgette Montose, I felt like someone had punched me in the stomach. They were both smiling as they looked down at the small device on the table. In one breath, I wanted to march over there, rip out all of Bridgette's hair, and stuff it down Lincoln's throat. In the next, I wanted to huddle in a corner and cry.

Feeling a splintering pain in my chest, I rushed from the lunchroom. I've never felt pain like that before.

He caught me at the end of the day getting on the bus and asked where I was at lunch. I was still hurting, so I lashed out and told him to go sit with Bridgette at the back. The pain on his face matched the pain I felt inside. Before he could say anything else, I stomped up the bus steps and took my regular seat, making sure to put my book bag in his spot to show him he wasn't invited to sit with me. I felt his anguished eyes on me as he walked by, but I continued to stare out the window.

I hated Bridgette, and he knew it. She always acted like she was better than everyone else and treated everyone like dirt, as though they were *beneath* her. I felt betrayed by him sitting with her at lunch. I don't know if he sat with her in the back of the bus. I only knew I missed having him beside me, even though I was the one who told him he couldn't.

"Molly?" he calls my name. I sniff and wipe away a tear from my cheek.

"I-I thought you wanted to sit with her," I whisper my fear. "I th-thought you liked her."

His face scrunches up like he ate something sour. "There's no way I could ever like a girl like Bridgette."

"You don't think she's pretty?"

He makes a gagging sound. "Definitely not. She's ugly. On the inside and out."

I look down at my hands fisted in my nightshirt. "I thought you wanted to make her your new girl."

His finger touches the underside of my chin, and he lifts my head.

"That'll never happen. I only have room for one girl, and that spot's already taken. It'll only ever be yours."

"Really?" Hope blossoms in my chest.

"Really." He smiles, and my world feels right again. "Forevermore."

"Forevermore," I breathe, and give him my own smile.

A bright light flashes outside the window, and I tense, waiting for the loud boom that's sure to follow. It comes three seconds later.

Lincoln steps so close to me I feel the heat of his body chase away the shivers in mine.

"Come on. I brought cards for us to play."

He's still wet from the rain, but I don't care as we climb on the bed. As if knowing exactly what I need, he drapes the blanket over both of us until we're huddled in our make-shift tent, facing each other. Storms are always easier to handle when Lincoln is with me. He somehow manages to keep the fear at bay.

He notices my journal sticking out from beneath my pillow and snatches it up, looking down at the cover. I've just started on my third one. Each time I fill one up, he gives me another with a new design on the cover. I don't worry about him opening it and reading what's inside. He's teased me about it before, but I trust him to not invade my privacy like that. Even so, he says the same thing he always says when he sees them.

"Tell me a story."

I always pick something from my journal when he asks that. I don't pick the real personal ones, ones that may be embarrassing. But I pick something that'll give him a glimpse into what I'm feeling, which always has something to do with him. After all, I stuck to my word when he gave me the first journal. It's filled with stories about him and me.

This time, I decided to retell the story of when I fell off my bike and scraped my knee about a year after we met. We were two blocks away from home, and he insisted on carrying me on his back. That day was special because it was then that I realized just how much he cared for me. The pain in his eyes reflected the same pain I felt from my scrape.

He smiles the whole time I talk, like hearing my voice is the sweetest sound to him.

"I almost went back to your house that night to smash your bike into bits," he confesses, smile still in place.

"Why in the world would you do that?"

He lifts a shoulder. "Because it was the stupid chain that made you fall. I hate anything that hurts you."

My insides turn to goo. Lincoln has always been protective of me. It's one of the many things I love about him.

I pull my knees to my chest and rest my chin on top of them. "You can't protect me from everything, Lincoln. I'm bound to get hurt sometimes."

He grunts. "You wanna bet?"

I shake my head and smile.

"I'm serious," he says, his smile gone. "There's not a thing I wouldn't do to protect you. You're my girl and my best friend, Molly. It hurts *me* when you hurt."

Thinking back, I remember all of the times I've been in some type of pain, whether it be from a scrape, a bruise, or my feelings hurt. Lincoln always looks like he's hurting too. I feel the same way with him. I hate the thought of him being in pain.

I stuff my journal back under my pillow. When I look back at him, he reaches out and pushes my hair away from my face.

"Why do you do that?" I ask curiously. He's done it a lot over the years, including the first day we met.

"Because your hair gets in the way of me seeing your pretty face. I like looking at you."

His words are spoken quietly, but the meaning behind them is loud and clear. The look in his eyes has something warm settling in my stomach and expanding to my chest.

I give him a shy smile and reach for the deck of cards.

We play game after game of Go Fish, War, and Rummy while the storm continues outside. Afterward, we end up falling asleep on my bed. Mom finds us on top of the covers, Lincoln on his back with me squished up to his side, as if seeking protection against the storm.

CHAPTER FIVE

LINCOLN
14 Years Old

I slip my hand into Molly's. It's different than all the other times we've held hands. Normally, it's just our palms pressed together with our fingers wrapped around the other's. This time though, I lace our fingers together. It feels better this way. Like we're somehow closer.

I turn my head and look at her. Her eyes are closed, the long, thick, auburn lashes resting against her cheeks. The freckles she despises so much scatter her face. Most of them are across her nose and cheeks, but there are a few that sprinkle the rest of her fair skin. She stopped wearing glasses a couple of months ago when she begged her mom to get her contacts. I won't tell her, but I miss seeing her wear them. Her nose, small and slightly tipped up at the end, has turned a slight pink from being in the sun today. And her lips—my eyes zero in on them—are a pretty pink, the bottom slightly plumper than the top. They look soft and smooth. For the last two years, I've wondered what they would feel like pressed against my own. How her tongue would feel sliding against mine. And how she would taste. Would she be sweet like the fruit stripe gum she likes to chew? Or minty like her toothpaste?

She's changed over the last few years, more so in the last twelve months. It's hard not to notice those changes. Her hips filling out, growing boobs, her face slimming, and losing her childlike features. All of them have played havoc with my own changing body. Puberty has been a killer.

There's a twitch in my jeans, so I force myself to think about something else.

"Did you have fun today?" I ask, keeping my head turned toward her.

We're both lying down on the thick grass in her backyard, so I can only see half of her face, but I know she's smiling because her lips curl up on this side. We've lain here like this many times over the last few years. Sometimes we watch the clouds and make animals out of them, and sometimes we look for shooting stars. It's sort of become our thing.

Today, six years ago, was the day we first met. It was the best day of my life.

"I did." She finally opens her eyes and turns her head, giving me access to her gorgeous green eyes. "Thank you for today. You made it so very special." She smiles. "But then again, every day with you is special."

To celebrate our friendship, we rode our bikes to all of our favorite places. And the places we couldn't get to on our bikes, my mom drove us.

I get up on my elbow and look down at her. "I plan to make every day with you special."

"I can't believe it's been six years already." Her eyes twinkle in the fading sunlight, and her red hair looks beautiful spread out on the grass. "What do you think we'll be doing six years from now?"

I know what we'll be doing, but there's a question of my own I want her to answer first.

I push back a few strands of hair from her cheek, my eyes sliding once more to her lips. I lick mine and bring my gaze back to hers, pleased to see her own eyes dart away from my mouth.

"Will you…." I clear my throat, nervous energy making my words come out a croak. "Will you go out with me, Molly? Will you be my girlfriend?"

Her eyes widen, and her lips part. She doesn't say anything at first, just stares up at me in wonderment. I know what her answer will be before she gives it. I've known from the first moment I saw her she'd one day be my girlfriend, even before I really knew what one was. And I know she knows that too. This is just a formality, really. We're already as close as two people our age could be. What we are is so much more than best friends, or boyfriend and girlfriend. We're two pieces of a whole. She's the beat of my heart, just as I'm the blood that rushes through her veins. We breathe life into each other.

Her lips curve up into a breathtaking smile and she breathes the one word, the only word, that makes my life more complete. "Yes."

I smile down at her. "Ask me your question again."

She giggles. "What do you think we'll be doing six years from now?"

I release her hand to cup her cheek, moving my thumb along her jaw to the corner of her tempting mouth.

"We'll be twenty then, so we'll both be in college." She nods, her eyes lighting up. We both already know what we want to do with our lives. I want to do something with art, and she wants to work with animals.

"But...." I lean over, putting our faces closer. Her warm breath fans across my face, and her green eyes darken. "There's something I want to do before then."

"What?" she whispers, her cheeks flushing an incredible pink.

I can practically feel her heart pumping in her chest, the rhythm matching my own rapid beat.

"Kiss you."

I lean down and settle my lips over hers for our first kiss.

Never in my wildest dreams could I have conjured up what kissing Molly would be like. She's the best thing I've ever tasted and the best thing I've ever felt. There's nothing, nowhere, I could compare it to. It's simply one of those things that's indescribable.

Her lips are soft and sweet, and when she opens her mouth to me, it's like I've died and gone to Heaven.

This isn't just our first kiss we've shared together; it's our first kiss we've shared with *anyone*. And knowing we'll both only ever kiss the other, makes it so much sweeter and more significant.

I touch the tip of my tongue to the tip of hers. Our mouths slide back and forth and side to side. Our heads twist and tilt and switch directions as we explore. We're clumsy, but neither cares, because it's still perfect. Everything we do, everything we are, is perfect. That's how it's always been and how it will always be.

I keep the kiss short, even though I'd love nothing more than to stay here all night doing exactly what we're doing. But I don't think being caught by her dad would go over well.

Lifting my head, I watch as Molly's eyes flutter open. The expression on her face—amazement and bliss—makes my heart jump in my chest. A small smile tips up her glistening lips, and her tongue darts out to rub along the bottom one, savoring my taste. I do the same.

Her hand twitches against my ribs. My jeans grow uncomfortably tight, but I ignore it. I've become a master at hiding my body's reaction to her.

"What now?" she asks quietly.

"Now, we start our life together."

She nods, accepting and agreeing with me. She's always felt it too, this kismet between us.

"Okay."

I lean down and kiss the tip of her nose before lying back

down. My arm goes around her shoulders, and she rests her head on my chest, snuggling against my side.

Together, we stare up at the darkening sky until the first streak of light flashes before us. More follow, and soon the sky is full of stars falling from the sky.

I make many wishes tonight, each one about the girl lying in my arms.

CHAPTER SIX

MOLLY
16 Years Old

Waves wash over Lincoln's and my bare feet as we walk down the beach hand in hand. We left our shoes by the soft dunes back a ways. The warm breeze and the salty air surrounds us, releasing a briny smell. The sun has started to set, making the horizon a beautiful pinkish purple. No one is ever on this part of the beach, which is the way I like it. It means Lincoln and I will be alone. It's not that I don't like being around others when Lincoln is with me. It's in this particular moment, I want him to myself.

The wind picks up, and I brush my hair over my shoulders. The thought to put it up doesn't even cross my mind. Lincoln once told me he loves my hair loose, so I try to keep it that way as much as possible to please him. It's funny because he likes my hair falling freely down my back, but he's constantly tucking it behind my ears so he can see my face. It's endearing.

We come across a small brown and white conch shell, but before I can scoop it up, he bends and grabs it first. After examining it for a moment, he drops it into the pocket of his cargo shorts. I wonder what plans he has for it.

I finger the little cockleshell necklace Lincoln made and gave me for Christmas one year. He's made me many things with the shells we find when we walk the beach: hair clips, an ankle bracelet, a candle, a nightlight. He's naturally artistic. There's no telling what he'll do with the conch shell, but I can't wait to find out. The necklace, though, is my favorite. It was the first shell we ever found together.

"What are you smiling so prettily about?" he asks, weaving us both around a piece of driftwood.

"Just wondering what you're going to make me with that shell," I answer honestly.

He lifts a brow and smirks, the look making his eyes dance in the fading light. "Maybe it's not for you."

My smile grows, both of us knowing I'll be getting whatever it is in a day or two. I've got a box full of things he's made me. Some I actually use, but some I keep hidden away, not wanting anything to happen to them. He makes things for his mom too, and even my mom, but the seashells he reserves only for me.

"Okay, hotshot. We'll see."

He laughs, and the sound sends a shot of pleasure to my stomach. His laugh is one of my favorite things to witness. His whole face lights up.

We come across a small alcove in a massive rock. Lincoln and I have come here several times. It's like our very own hiding spot. The rest of the world fades away when we're inside alone.

He helps me over a few of the larger rocks. I keep my eyes down to see where I'm going. I glance around in awe when I notice the lit candles, red flower petals on the rock floor, the picnic basket, and the make-shift bed made out of thick blankets sitting right in the middle of our little paradise.

I spin around and meet his eyes. He's a few feet behind me with his hands stuffed in his pockets. His eyes nervously flicker back and forth between mine.

"This is beautiful, Lincoln. I can't believe you did all this."

He shrugs like it's no big deal, but to me it is.

Most teenagers our age have already had sex or are doing the cliché thing and waiting for prom night. We've done pretty much everything else, but we've never discussed when we would go all the way. We only knew we didn't want to be like everyone else. We wanted it to be special and not rushed because it was the cool thing to do. We both knew this night was coming, just not when and where. I don't think Lincoln could have picked a better place and time.

"Are you okay?" he asks, stepping toward me.

I give him a genuine smile. "More than okay."

Yesterday he told me he had a surprise for me. No matter how much I begged him to tell me what it was, he held steady, keeping his secret close. But, somehow, I knew when he brought me here, this would be the night.

He wraps his big hands around my small waist, gently pulling me forward until our chests are lightly pressed together.

I've always loved the feeling of Lincoln against me. We're like a puzzle, fitting together perfectly.

Lacing his fingers through my hair on one side, he pushes the strands back, leaving his palm at the back of my head. "Are you sure this is what you want? We can just have dinner and lie down for a while."

I rest my hand on his chest, feeling the hard thump of his heart, and use the other to cup his cheek. "Just as I am with everything to do with you, I'm absolutely sure. I want this more than anything in the world, Lincoln. I want you to love me."

One side of his mouth tips up, and he bends to nip the tip of my nose. "I already do love you."

"I know you do, but I want you to love my body. More specifically, *make love* to my body."

I can already feel the swell of his erection against my lower stomach, and it sends a shot of adrenaline through me. I'm nervous, because hey, what girl wouldn't be their first time? But I'm also anxious. So anxious, I'm shaking.

"Are you scared?" he whispers the question as he pulls me completely flush against him.

I shake my head slowly. "Not scared. I could never be scared with you." I run my fingers through the back of his hair and peek at him through my lashes. "Just excited."

He gives me the smirk I always love. "Excited, huh?"

"Definitely."

He bends his head and presses his lips against mine. I open to him immediately. Any time Lincoln and I are together, something beautiful settles inside me. My heart beats steady and strong, like it's not whole and fully functioning until he's near.

I wrap my arms around his neck, and the next thing I know, I'm lifted off the ground. My legs wrap around his waist, and the amazing friction of having him so close has a moan breaking from my lips. From the hiss that leaves Lincoln's lips and the tightening of his hands on my butt, I know it feels just as good to him.

With our mouths still fused together, Lincoln carries me over to the make-shift bed. He carefully drops to his knees and lays me down. The soft material of the blankets meet my back. In the next second, I'm surrounded by his comforting warmth again.

He undresses me slowly, the admiration in his eyes as he reveals each part of my body making me feel more beautiful and cherished than I've ever felt before.

When he takes his own clothes off, I can't help but stare in amazement at him. We've both seen each other naked, but each time I see his magnificent body, I'm astounded that he's actually mine. Lincoln is beautiful in mind, body, and spirit, and I feel blessed beyond measure he wants to share his life with me.

We make love, and I swear it has to be the sweetest kind of love there ever was. He praises me with his words, calling me beautiful over and over again. He's attentive, kind, and worships my body like it's a shrine. Then he allows me to do the same to him.

It's perfect, just as I knew it would be with Lincoln.

Afterward, we lie beneath one of the thinner blankets, my head on his chest and him playing with my hair. Goosebumps pop up my arms when some of the strands tickle my side.

I tilt my head back so I can see his handsome face.

"Thank you," I whisper softly. "I never knew something could be so beautiful."

He rolls to his side, making sure to keep his arm under my head. His hand settles against my waist, and I can't help the little shiver the touch causes. My eyes melt in the gray pools of his.

"It was only beautiful because it was you and me."

"I wonder if it'll be like that every time," I muse.

His hand begins to trail up and down my back. "Better. Every time will be better than the last."

I smile and place my hand on his chest where his heart is. "That's hard to believe. This time was perfect in every way."

Even the slight pinch of pain when he first entered me was perfect because I knew it was leading up to something even better. I've heard some of my friends say the first time isn't the greatest, that practice makes perfect, but I can't imagine it getting better than what we just did.

I snuggle up closer to Lincoln, placing my ear against his sternum so I can hear his heart beating.

"I love you, Lincoln." Although I say the words quietly, my voice carries throughout the alcove.

"I love you too, Molly," he answers, his voice echoing. "Forevermore."

I smile and close my eyes. "Forevermore."

CHAPTER SEVEN

MOLLY
17 Years Old

I rub my hands together then stuff them in my armpits as I wait for Lincoln to come out of the theater. It's cold out, much colder than when we went in a couple of hours ago. I brought a light jacket because I knew the temperature was dropping, but I didn't think it was supposed to get this cold.

Leaning against the wall in hopes of blocking the frigid wind, I look up and down the street. It's a weeknight, so most people in Barre Vale are already tucked safely in their warm homes. Lincoln and I decided at the last minute to go to the theater and watch a late show. We were the only people in the theater, which made it perfect for making out.

My cheeks flush, and a smile touches my lips as I remember

what Lincoln did to me with his hands and mouth. I'm going to have to wear a scarf to cover my neck for the next week.

Raucous laughter catches my attention. My already cold breath freezes in my lungs when I spot Mark and Jensen walking down the sidewalk toward me. They haven't noticed me yet, but I know it's only a matter of time. I peek my head around the brick building toward the entrance of the theater, hoping I can either make a dash for the door before they get to me or spot someone inside in case this goes sour. I've only had to deal with the duo a couple of times since Lincoln rescued me from them on the playground all those years ago, but I've seen the looks they give me when he's not around. For some unknown reason, they hate me.

"Well, look who it is," Jensen taunts, and I realize I've lost my chance to dash to the door. I still try, though, but I don't get far before Mark blocks my way.

"Where ya goin', pretty Molly?" he asks, running his eyes up and down my body like I'm some treat he's waiting to devour.

Disgust and loathing twist together in my stomach.

"Leave me alone," I demand, taking a step back from Mark.

"Where's your boyfriend?" Jensen asks.

"In the bathroom," I answer. "He'll be out here any minute, so I suggest you both leave before he does."

Mark snorts and hits Jensen's arm with the back of his hand. "She makes it sound like we should be scared of Lincoln."

Jensen tips his head back and laughs. When he brings his head back down, the look in his eyes and the way he grins leeringly at me has shivers racing down my spine. He steps forward, but before I have a chance to dart away, his arm is locked around my waist, and I'm forced against his chest.

His breath smells like tobacco and something rotten. "What in the hell kind of special pussy do you possess to have Lincoln wrapped so tight around your finger?" He sniffs my cheek. "Whatever it is, I want some of it."

Bile rises in my throat, and I'm seconds away from puking all over him when he picks me up and starts walking around the corner. I struggle, pushing my hands against his chest and kicking my legs, but he's too strong. My scream is cut short when Mark slaps his hand over my mouth.

"Don't worry, sugar. We're only going to have a little fun. Once we're done, we'll give you back to your pussy-whipped boyfriend."

I'm just set on my feet behind a dumpster and spun around to face a brick wall when a loud growl comes from somewhere. Feet pound on the pavement seconds before the body at my back is no longer there. I spin around, my eyes wide with fright, and take in the scene. Bones crack against bones as Lincoln lands a punch on Jensen's face. Jensen stumbles back, holding his hand to his nose. Bright blood gushes between his fingers.

Mark charges Lincoln, but he's not quick enough, or maybe it's because Lincoln has more of a reason to fight him off. Just before Mark's shoulder meets Lincoln's stomach, Lincoln steps to the side and clips Mark on the side of the head. It catches him off guard, and he falls to his knees. Lincoln takes advantage and rams his boot into his face.

The fight is over before it really had a chance to begin. Jensen and Mark have always been scared of Lincoln. I don't know what they saw on his face that day on the playground, but they normally avoid him, only taunting me when he's not around, which isn't often.

With an evil look that says he wishes Lincoln would drop dead, and blood dripping from his now crooked nose, Jensen walks over to Mark, grabs him by the arm, and yanks him up. Neither says a word as they stomp off around the corner of the building.

The moment they're gone, Lincoln's heated gaze whips to me. His expression morphs from irate to concern immediately.

"Are you okay?" he asks, moving to me as fast as his legs can carry him. His hands frame my face, and he looks me over from head to toe, checking for injuries.

"I'm fine." My voice is unsteady, so I try to strengthen it for Lincoln's benefit. "Just a little shaken up."

His jaw ticks, and he darts a glance over his shoulder where Jensen and Mark disappeared. "I should have broken their arms and legs," he growls, bringing his eyes back to me.

I cup one of his cheeks and bring his face closer to mine. "No, you shouldn't have. What you *did* do was good enough. I don't think they would have taken it far. They were just trying to scare me."

I honestly don't know how far they would have taken it. It scares me to even contemplate what they're really capable of. But if I don't want Lincoln to be arrested for assault, I need him to believe they would have stopped before things got too carried away.

I roll to my toes and press my lips against his, trying to distract him from going after the assholes. "Thank you."

He pulls his mouth away but presses his forehead against mine. “Never thank me for protecting you. I’ll always be there to protect my girl.”

I smile, and despite the situation, my heart flutters. No matter what’s going on around us, Lincoln never has to work hard to bring a smile to my face. It’s one of the many reasons why I love him.

I shiver when a gust of wind whips around us. Lincoln tears off his zip-up hoodie and lays it over my shoulders.

“What about you?” He ignores my question as he threads my arms through the armholes. “You’ll be left in only a T-shirt.”

He zips it up, and for good measure, brings the hood over my head. Angling his face toward mine, he kisses me softly. “I’ll be okay, baby. Now let’s get you home.”

CHAPTER EIGHT

LINCOLN

18 Years Old

I stand with my hands tightly clasped in front of me, my nerves making me shift from one foot to the other. All eyes are pointed at me, but mine are glued to the back of the church as I anxiously wait. This is the day I feel like I've waited for my entire life. The day I finally make Molly mine in the only way I haven't already.

Soft murmurs and shuffles sound throughout the room filled with our families and friends. Hundreds of pretty white dahlia flowers decorate the space. The wedding hasn't even started yet, and I can already hear the sniffles coming from Mom. Molly's mom isn't doing much better. They'll both be a blubbering mess before it's over.

A hand lands on my shoulder from behind and squeezes the tense muscle.

"Dude, relax," Owen, my best man, says quietly. "There's no way in hell that girl isn't showing up for this. I don't know who's more in love with whom. You or her."

I flick my gaze to him for a brief moment, before putting it back on the door Molly will be coming through any minute.

"I'm not worried if she'll show or not—I know she will. I'm just wondering how I'm going to stop myself from walking down the aisle, scooping her into my arms, and running back up here."

The officiant chokes out a laugh as Owen chuckles. They both think I'm joking, but I couldn't be more serious. From the time I recognized what love was, I knew it was leading to this point. We're both only eighteen years old and on our way to college. But while our parents may have wished we'd wait until we were older, we felt there was no reason to. Our getting married was inevitable.

"Not to worry, I'll make sure to keep you right here," Owen snickers.

I grunt. Due to the inappropriateness of the time and place, I refrain from flipping him off.

The room quiets down when the first strings of the song Molly and I chose comes across the speakers. Instead of the traditional Canon in D music, we opted for one of our favorite songs. The soft strings of "*I Knew I Loved You*" by Savage Garden begins to play.

Lindsay, Molly's ten-year-old sister and flower girl, appears first. She's cute as hell in her white dress with pink stitched flowers covering the skirt. With each step she takes, she reaches into the basket she's holding and drops a few pink flower petals on the floor in front of her. When she reaches the end, she goes to sit beside her mom in the front row.

Behind her, Zoey, one of Molly's friends, steps into the doorway. Her arm is tucked into Landon's, Molly's cousin. Both smile as they walk slowly down the aisle. All eyes follow them, but I keep mine pointed to the back.

A new couple appears. Sabastian and Rosalie, friends of Molly and me. The look in Sabs' eyes says he knows exactly what the waiting is doing to me, and he finds it hilarious. Once they reach the end of the aisle, they break apart in front of me to go stand beside Zoey and Landon.

One more person to go. One more person to watch walk down the aisle before I can see the one person who matters the most.

Molly's best friend and maid of honor appears, white and purple bouquet in hand. I'm mostly a patient and laid back man, but I swear it takes Jenna forever before she's standing in front of me. Instead of taking her place beside the bridesmaids, she steps closer. Her eyes shine with tears, and her smile is wobbly.

"She's beautiful, Lincoln," she voices quietly. "I have absolutely no doubt you both will be very happy together."

My throat tightens, and I give her a jerky nod. Her words ring true in my head. Not because she said them, but because I know in my gut Molly and I *will* be happy.

When I look back at the doorway, the girl of my dreams, my soul mate, my kismet, my *everything*, is standing there. All the air in my lungs rushes out on a long breath, and I'm left standing there momentarily dizzy from the effect. There are no words to describe the stunningly gorgeous woman staring at me. Nothing could have prepared me for the overwhelming emotions I would feel seeing her like this.

Beautiful, sleeveless, white dress that molds to her breasts, long white skirts that flow flawlessly to the floor, striking red hair pulled up with soft tendrils framing her freckled cheeks, veil trailing behind her, and hypnotic green eyes set only on me.

She smiles, and it's only then that I can breathe again.

She takes her first step with her father beside her, and my heart hammers in my chest. I ball my hands into fists, pressing them against my thighs. A nearly uncontrollable need to run to her grips me. As if sensing my turmoil, Owen's hand lands on my shoulder. I take a deep breath and blow it out slowly.

Neither one of us looks away as she walks toward me and the life we're destined to share.

After what seems like a thousand minutes, Molly and her father stop in front of me. She turns to her dad, her smile turning watery. Leaning down, he places a kiss on her cheek before they face me again.

"Who gives this woman to be married to this man?" the officiant asks.

"I do," Douglas responds, his voice strong and sure.

He takes one of Molly's manicured hands and offers it to me. I'm surprised to see my own hand shaking as I reach out, but as soon as her palm is nestled into mine, it stops. Everything stops. Time, the whole world, and everything in it, except Molly and me.

I barely hear anything after that. All I can focus on is her and how beautiful she is and how lucky I am to have her.

I don't know how many minutes pass, but the officiant clears his throat, and I reluctantly switch my gaze to him.

He addresses the crowd. "Molly and Lincoln have decided to share a few words."

I set my eyes back on Molly and smile. "Tell me a story."

Her answering smile is radiant.

"There once was a boy on a playground, who saved a girl from some bullies. From the first moment she saw the boy's beautiful, gray eyes, she was utterly captivated. She didn't realize it at the time, but that was the day she met the boy who would become her happily ever after, her destiny."

A single tear slides down her cheek, and I swipe it away with my thumb.

"From that moment on, the girl and boy were inseparable. There wasn't anything that could pull them apart. They were best friends first, then they became lovers. Now, from this day forward, they'll love, honor, and cherish each other as husband and wife. Forevermore."

The only thing that can be heard in the room are quiet sniffles as people wipe their eyes. My own eyes sting, and I have to work really damn hard at keeping my emotions in check.

Going against tradition, I lean down and kiss Molly. It's a simple kiss, but it still holds an insurmountable amount of meaning.

Owen coughs from behind me, and I grudgingly pull away.

"I love you," I murmur for her ears only.

"I love you too, Lincoln." She smiles, and I smile back. Her eyes sparkle in the church's bright light. "Tell me a story."

My smile becomes a goofy grin. I'm usually the only one who requests a story, but for our wedding, we decided we would both share a glimpse of our past.

I lock our fingers together tighter and step so close the tips of my shoes touch the tips of her heels.

"Nothing in my life could have prepared me for you, Molly," I begin gruffly. "Everything has a reason for being, and you are mine. Without you, there is no me. The day I saw you on that playground, was the day my life began. I was only eight, but even then, I knew you were my kismet. My love for you is boundless, endless, and timeless. It won't end when I cease to exist, it'll only grow stronger. Every day since that first one on the playground, has been the best days of my life, and I promise that all of the tomorrows we share will be the best days of yours."

Her lips tremble, and more tears leak down her cheeks. I want nothing more than to pull her into my arms and forget about the crowded church behind us.

The officiant continues with his speech, and Molly and I exchange our vows, promising to love and cherish each other from this day forward. I slide the gold band with tiny sparkling diamonds on Molly's finger, and she does the same to mine with the matching band.

"I now pronounce you husband and wife," the officiant says loud and clear. "You may kiss the bride."

The words have barely passed his lips before I'm pulling

Molly forward. She fits perfectly against me as I wrap my arms around her waist and her arms band around my neck. This kiss is more than it should be in front of a crowd, but I couldn't care less. This woman is now my wife, and I want the whole world to know it.

When we pull back, both of our gazes are dazed. Her pale cheeks carry a light pinkish hue, and it makes me proud that I put it there. The fireflies I love so much are in her eyes again.

"Forevermore," she whispers.

"Forevermore," I repeat our promise back to her.

Gripping her hand, we turn and face our family and friends as Mr. and Mrs. Bradshaw.

CHAPTER NINE

MOLLY

22 Years Old

Gripping the little white stick with a shaky hand, I open my eyes and look down. A smile instantly spreads across my face, and my whole body fills with giddy happiness. I laugh as tears of joy slide down my cheeks.

It's silly, but I leave the bathroom twirling and dancing across the carpeted bedroom floor. My dance ends in front of the tall mirror in the corner, and my eyes move to my mid-section. Lifting my shirt, I stare at the smooth, flat surface of my stomach. My heart is incredibly full when I think about how it'll soon grow round. Many women dread the weight they'll gain and the inevitable stretch marks that will forever mark their body. Not me. I can't wait for those milestones.

I flatten my hand over my lower stomach, right where the tiny being Lincoln and I lovingly created is tucked inside. My cheeks hurt from grinning so much.

"Hey there, little bean," I say softly to the baby. "I already can't wait to meet you."

I hear the front door close, but I keep my focus on my stomach. I can't stop looking at it.

"Hey." Lincoln appears in the doorway. "I got you the...." His voice trails off when he sees me in front of the mirror. "Everything okay?"

I move my gaze from my stomach and meet Lincoln's eyes through the mirror. His expression turns to concern when he sees the tears on my cheeks.

"Everything is absolutely perfect."

It's then that he notices my shirt is pulled up, and one of my hands is laying protectively over my tummy. His eyes jerk back to mine, and he stalks across the room, stopping directly in front of me.

"Please tell me this is what I think it is?" he pleads, gripping my hips in his big hands.

I smile, and the force of my nod has more tears falling down my cheeks.

"I'm pregnant. *We're* pregnant."

"Holy shit," he breathes and drops his eyes to my stomach.

In the next moment, he's down on his knees in front of me, lifting my shirt higher. His hands are shaking as he gently runs the tips of his fingers over the area right above my pubic bone.

"There's a baby in here. *Our* baby," he states huskily.

"Yes." I run my fingers through his hair. "I still have to confirm it with the doctor, but I did five tests just to be sure."

Lincoln had no idea I bought the tests. I wanted to wait until I saw the results before I told him, so I didn't get his hopes up.

"I can't believe it. We made a baby. A little blend of Molly and Lincoln." He looks up and grins at me, his eyes shining. "We made a Molcoln."

I laugh and shake my head at the silly man. "Well, it would certainly explain my weird cravings lately."

Dropping his eyes back to my belly, he leans forward and places the gentlest of kisses against my skin.

"You're going to be the most beautiful baby the world has ever seen," he whispers quietly to my stomach. "And we're going to spoil you rotten. You'll get everything you ever want. If you want the world, I'll find a way to give it to you. If you want the stars, I'll steal a spaceship and go pluck them from the sky. Nothing is the limit."

I giggle at his playfulness, loving the way he already adores our child. "You may be taking fatherhood a little too far already."

"Nope. There is no taking fatherhood too far. I want to be the best father any child has ever had."

I cup his cheeks and bring his head up so I can see his face. "You're already the best father a child could have. Our baby will be lucky to have you."

He grabs one of my hands and kisses the center of my palm, then leans forward and presses one more to my stomach before he stands.

"We'll both be lucky. And I have no doubt this baby will be more loved than any other in existence."

Tears spring to my eyes. This man—this kind, gentle, and caring man—is more than I could ever have hoped for. Not for the first time, and it won't be the last, I send up a thank you to the heavens above for sending me Lincoln.

CHAPTER TEN

LINCOLN
23 Years Old

"You're doing great, baby. You've got this," I tell Molly and brush away the damp hair on her forehead. "You're almost done. We're almost there."

The tight grip she has on my hand hurts like hell, but I don't stop her from squeezing it. She could rip my hand off if she wanted to, and I'd let her.

"All right, Molly, give me one more big push," Dr. Becker coaxes.

Baring her teeth, Molly lets out a low moan as her face turns red and scrunches up as she gives a final push. Once she's done, she relaxes back against the pillows in exhaustion, her eyes red and barely open. It kills me to see her in so much pain.

A loud piercing scream hits the air, and we both look up just as the doctor holds up a pink, squirming baby.

"Congratulations. You're now proud parents to a baby boy," Dr. Becker announces. "Daddy, would you like to cut the cord?"

My throat is too tight to say anything, so all I do is nod.

I press a kiss to Molly's forehead. "I'm proud of you," I murmur. "So damn proud."

Her smile is lazy but filled with so much love.

I'm nervous as hell when I walk to the end of the bed where the doctor is waiting for me. Our baby looks so tiny in his hands, and for a moment, my nervousness turns to fear. He looks so frail and fragile. He'll look even smaller in my bigger hands. What if something happens to him? What if I'm not a good father? What if I drop him or hold him too tight?

I push the thoughts away, refusing to let them take root, and take my first good look at my son. He's pink and covered in red and white chunks of something. His face is scrunched up as he screams his displeasure to the world. His hands, so damn tiny, are balled into little fists as he waves his arms around frantically.

He is, without a doubt, the most beautiful thing I've ever seen.

With a trembling hand, I grab the scissors one of the nurses holds out to me.

"You'll want to cut between the two clamps," the doctor instructs.

"It won't hurt him, will it?"

He chuckles. "No. He won't feel a thing."

Feeling like I'm on auto-pilot, I open the scissors, place the open blades to the spot on the grayish cord the doctor showed me, and squeeze them together. I'm surprised at how tough it is to cut through the cord. It's like cutting through a piece of thick, wet rope.

Watery looking blood seeps from the two ends, dripping onto the pad on the floor at the end of the bed. A nurse comes over, takes the scissors, and places them on the metal tray, before holding out a cloth. Dr. Becker wraps the blanket around the baby, wiping away some of the chunks and liquid off his face, before smiling at me.

"Would you like to take him to Momma to hold for a couple of minutes before we clean him?"

I stare at him wide-eyed, still in a daze from the delivery and cutting the cord. I jerk my eyes away from the doctor and stare at my son again. Pulling in a deep, calming breath, I hold out my arms, and the doctor settles him against my chest, showing me how to properly support his head.

The backs of my eyes sting, and I couldn't stop the tears from flowing down my cheeks if my life depended on it. A feeling of immense love fills my heart the moment he's in my arms. I thought I loved him when Molly was slowly growing him in her belly, but nothing could compare to what I feel right now. It's all-consuming, and the purest kind of love a person could have.

I walk slowly until I'm standing beside Molly. Taking care, I place him on her chest. Tears leak down her cheeks. Not from the pain of labor, but the insurmountable love she feels for our child. She stares down at him in awe.

"He's so beautiful," she whispers. "I can't believe he's ours."

Leaning down, I put my face close to hers as we both stare at the tiny person we created together. I run my finger down his little nose and grin when he snuggles closer to his mother's chest, like he's seeking her warmth and comfort.

"Welcome to the world, Lincoln Graham Bradshaw Junior. Your momma and daddy love you so much and are so happy to finally meet you."

He releases a big yawn and smacks his gummy lips together. There's a small dent in one cheek that looks like it might be a dimple, just like his mom's. I'm utterly transfixed when his eyes open, revealing a set of beautiful, dark-blue orbs. I don't know if he can actually see us or if we're just shadowy blobs to him, but I'd swear there's interest in his gaze. As if he's just as curious about us as we are about him.

Dr. Becker said that a lot of babies are born with blue eyes, but they can change over the first six to eight months after they are born. I wonder if our son's will change. Will they be a beautiful green like his mother's, or a stormy gray like mine?

"He's perfect, isn't he?"

I kiss her temple and murmur, "Absolutely perfect. You did good, Molly."

She looks at me, the little fireflies sparkling brighter than they ever have before. "We both did good."

"All right, Mom and Dad. It's time for Junior here to have his bath," a nurse says with a tender smile.

Disappointment settles in Molly's features, and I feel the same way. We only just had our son, and now the nurse is taking him away.

He receives a kiss from both of us before Molly reluctantly

hands him over to the nurse. I lay my forehead against her damp one.

"Thank you for giving me this special gift."

She cups my cheeks, and her eyes fall closed. "Thank you for choosing me to give it to you."

"I'll choose you for the rest of my days, Molly. Never doubt that."

She smiles. "I won't, because I'll choose you for the rest of mine."

CHAPTER ELEVEN

MOLLY

24 Years Old

Excitement courses through me as the realtor guides us around the beautiful house. This is the third one we've looked at today and the ninth one we've looked at this week. I knew the moment we pulled into the driveway and saw the outside, this was the one. Viewing the inside only solidified my thought. It's more perfect than I could have imagined. Four bedrooms, two and a half baths, a family room, living room, dining room, and a gorgeous kitchen. The property itself is beautiful and big, with the backyard fenced in. The icing on the cake is the massive building that comes with it. I can already envision Lincoln using it for his prospering art business. It's actually his art that's allowing us to buy a house. He's sold enough pieces that we have a nice chunk of change in the bank for a decent down payment.

The house we're renting now is great, but it's barely big enough for the three of us. After I finish vet school, in a little over a year, we want to try for another baby. We'll need the extra room when that happens. Not to mention, Lincoln's business is growing, and he needs the room for his art equipment.

We've just been shown the master bedroom when I spin around and face Lincoln. The realtor stepped out into the hallway when she got a phone call. "What do you think?" I can't keep the excitement out of my voice.

He smiles and tucks a piece of hair behind my ear. "I can tell by the huge grin on your face that *you* like it."

My grin grows bigger. "I do. I love it actually and think it's perfect. But you have to love it too."

"I was hoping you liked it because I do too." He looks around the room, taking in the big space, before dropping his eyes back to me. His brows jump playfully, and his voice lowers. "I can just imagine making love to you in our bed over there."

I giggle, a thrill racing through me. "Or maybe right here." I look down at our feet. "During those times when we get impatient and never make it to the bed."

His expression turns hungry and he palms my bottom. "I like the way you think, Mrs. Bradshaw." He dips down for a kiss. It's interrupted when we hear the realtor ending her call. "So, are we doing this?"

"Yes!" I jump up and wrap my arms around his neck and my legs around his waist.

Lincoln spins us around when we hear laughter from behind us.

"You two are so cute," the realtor says, smiling indulgently. She holds up her phone. "That was a call from the office." Her smile drops fractionally. "Unfortunately, another couple just made an offer on this place. The good news is, it's for the asking price. If you're willing to offer a bit more, I think the owners would accept, but we have to move quickly."

I look at Lincoln, my expression hopeful. The second he sees the question in my eyes, he turns back to the realtor. "Offer ten grand over the asking price."

"Yah!" She claps her hands, a wide smile stretching across her face. "I'll get it in as soon as we leave here. We should hear something back within a couple of days." She turns to exit the room but spins back around in the doorway. "Oh! I forgot to show you the attic." Using the hand holding her phone, she throws her thumb over her shoulder. "Would you like to take a look?"

Lincoln and I look at each other. Seeing the attic won't change our mind, but we're already here, so we may as well look anyway.

"Sure," he answers.

We follow her out into the hallway where she grabs a long string hanging from the ceiling. The stairs creak as they descend. She climbs up the ladder first, I follow behind her, and Lincoln takes up the rear.

It's dark up here, but thankfully, the realtor finds the cord for the light. The single bulb doesn't help much, but it gives just enough light to show us how big the area is. Attics are notoriously creepy, but I don't get that weird vibe. If anything, I feel a sense of calm, which is strange in itself.

Stepping away from Lincoln, I look around the empty space. Or rather, the space that's supposed to be empty. Off in a darkened corner, I notice several stacks of boxes.

"What are those?" I ask the realtor.

I feel Lincoln come up behind me. "Did the owners leave them behind?"

"No. The owners said they were up here when they bought the house, but they never messed with them. Not sure why." She steps up beside us. "I can have them removed if you buy the place."

For some unknown reason, I turn to the realtor and say, "If it's okay with you, I'd like to leave them."

She shrugs. "Okay."

I don't know why, but the thought of someone removing them doesn't sit well with me. Actually, it leaves me jittery.

"You guys ready to get the ball rolling?" the realtor asks, taking the first step down the ladder.

Turning away from the mysterious boxes, I flash her a big grin. "We are." I turn my grin to Lincoln. "Let's go win our house."

CHAPTER TWELVE

MOLLY
28 Years Old

Stepping outside on the back porch, a smile breaks out across my face at the sight before me. Gray, a shortened version of his middle name, has had his daddy wrapped around his little finger from the moment Lincoln held him in his arms. The bond between the two is beautiful and unbreakable. I could spend hours simply watching them together.

Lincoln is on his hands and knees with Gray on his back, giving him a horseback ride around the yard.

"Faster, Daddy!" Gray calls eagerly, his smile so big his eyes are squinted almost shut.

I laugh. Poor Lincoln is trying his best, but really, how fast can you go on your hands and knees? He absolutely refuses to disappoint our son though, so despite the pain he's surely feeling in his knees, he moves faster.

Grabbing hold of the railing, I waddle down the steps, deciding to give my husband a reprieve. I stop for a moment and suck in a breath when a pinch of pain stabs at my back. Damn Braxton Hicks are killer this go around. They've been coming off and on the last couple of days. I haven't told Lincoln, or he'd freak out and shove me in the car to go to the hospital. He doesn't handle it well when I'm in pain

"Hey, you two."

"Momma! Momma!" Gray screeches when he sees me. He holds out his arms for me to pick him up, but before I get the chance, Lincoln does some weird maneuver where he flips around but manages to catch Gray before he can fall to the ground. He's on his feet standing in front of me a second later, Gray's butt settled on his arm.

Gray reaches for me again and wraps his little arms around my neck. I get as close to the pair as I can and snuggle my face against his tiny shoulder.

Gray may be a daddy's boy, but he still adores his momma.

"Hey, bud, you know Momma can't hold you right now," Lincoln says gently.

Gray pulls back and leans over to pat my stomach. "'Cause my sister's in dere, and I'm too heavy for Momma now."

I hate that I can't hold Gray. I'm only a week away from my due date, and Lincoln has been a bear the last several weeks about me carrying heavy stuff. I keep telling him I'll be fine, but he won't be persuaded.

"That's right, but as soon as Gemma is here, your momma will hold you a bunch," Lincoln reassures him.

"And I can hold Gemma." His gorgeous gray eyes look at me for confirmation.

I rub my nose against his. "You sure can."

"Yah!" He claps his hands in excitement, making Lincoln and me laugh.

He starts to wiggle to be put down, so after a kiss to his cheek, Lincoln sets him on his feet. The sun has settled behind the horizon, and the fireflies are starting to come out. He takes off to try and catch one. We come outside at dusk a lot this time of year because Gray loves to play with them. Lincoln and I did the same when we were kids, and we wanted our children to enjoy it too. Of course, we always make sure he doesn't hold them too tightly for too long, so they can find their mates.

Lincoln wraps his arms around me from behind and settles his hands over my stomach. Gemma uses that moment to kick his hand. Goosebumps pop up on my arms when his breath fans across my neck from his chuckle.

"She's going to be feisty," he says with a chuckle.

"She's only anxious to get out and see the world."

"She's not the only one ready for her to get out."

I place my hands over Lincoln's and lean my head against his chest. We're silent as we listen to Gray squeal as he chases the fireflies. These are the times I cherish the most, watching our son so happy and carefree.

"Momma! Daddy! Look! I caught one!" He comes dashing over as fast as his little five-year-old legs will carry him. Stopping in front of us, he holds out his hands. They're cupped together as big as he can get them without letting the bug get free.

I bend over to take a look, while Lincoln goes to his knees. Gray's grin is big as he slowly opens his hands. A light flashes, and the bug crawls across his palm.

"It tickles." He giggles. God, I love that sound.

The backyard begins to sparkle and come to life with more tiny flashing lights.

"It's time to let him go," I tell him.

He nods with all seriousness a five-year-old can have. "He's gotta find his bes frien."

"That's right."

Lincoln and I share a soft look, and I know he's remembering when I came up with the idea when we were kids.

Gray turns around and holds his hand up as high as he can. His grin is back as the firefly takes flight off his hand. Lincoln scoops him up with one arm and wraps the other around my waist. Rising to my toes, I lay a chaste kiss against my big man's lips, then turn to my little man and do the same.

The three of us turn and watch the beautiful display the fireflies give us until they slowly trickle away as they find their 'best friends.'

Another pain hits my back, this time moving around to my stomach. It's so sharp that I bend over, and a moan forces its way past my lips. I clutch my stomach, feeling the tightness.

"Molly!" Lincoln's loud voice has me looking at him. He's set Gray on his feet, and he's kneeling down in front of me. Worry lines his face, and all I want to do is smooth it away. Until another stabbing pain hits. "Goddamnit, Molly. Talk to me, baby."

"It hurts," I moan once the pain fades some. I begin to pant. "Like really freaking hurts."

A rush of warmth slides down my legs. Lincoln notices right away, his eyes widening in surprise before fear takes its place.

Lifting my dress to my knees, I look down. Worry has me gasping when I notice the trails of red running rivers down my legs. It's not supposed to be so red. Why in the hell is it so red?

"Lincoln?" My bottom lip wobbles as tears cascade down my cheeks. "That's not normal, right?" Another cramp comes, and I bite my tongue to keep from crying out. "Something's wrong."

One minute I'm hunched over, the next I'm cradled in Lincoln's arms, and he's striding across the yard.

"Gray!" he yells. "Come on, Son!"

Through my tears, over Lincoln's shoulder, I watch as Gray runs on his little legs after us toward the back door. His gray eyes, so much like his father's, look frightened. I want to scoop him up and hug him, tell him everything will be okay. But I'm scared it won't be. There's too much blood, and the pain is different than the last time. Something feels terribly wrong.

"I'm scared, Lincoln," I whisper, clutching his shoulders.

"Everything's going to be okay," he says, his jaw clenched. "It's got to be okay, baby."

Another pain grips me, this one worse than the last, and I can't help the small cry that leaves my lips.

"Get the door for me, Gray," Lincoln says calmly. One look

at his face says he's anything but calm. He's trying his best though, for Gray's sake.

"What's wrong with Mommy?" Gray asks. It breaks my heart when I see the tears in his eyes.

Lincoln stops and turns to face our son. The struggle to pick Gray up and comfort him is written all over his face.

"Momma's okay," he tells him hoarsely. "Your little sister is coming, so we need to take Momma to the hospital. Can you get my keys from the counter and open the door for me?"

He nods and dashes away. A moment later, the jingle of keys flashes by us as he runs to the door. A moment after that, Lincoln is setting me down in the passenger seat and buckling me in, making sure the strap goes under my belly. As he closes the door and gets Gray situated in his car seat, another wave of pain comes. I ball my hands into fists and suck in a sharp breath.

Seconds later, Lincoln's behind the wheel and backing out of the driveway. His eyes flicker down to my dress and the blood coating it. Reaching over, he grabs my hand. I can feel his trembling as he brings mine to his lips. Seeing the tears in his eyes scares me more than anything because I know he knows something is wrong too.

I close my eyes and send up a silent prayer.

Please let my baby girl be okay.

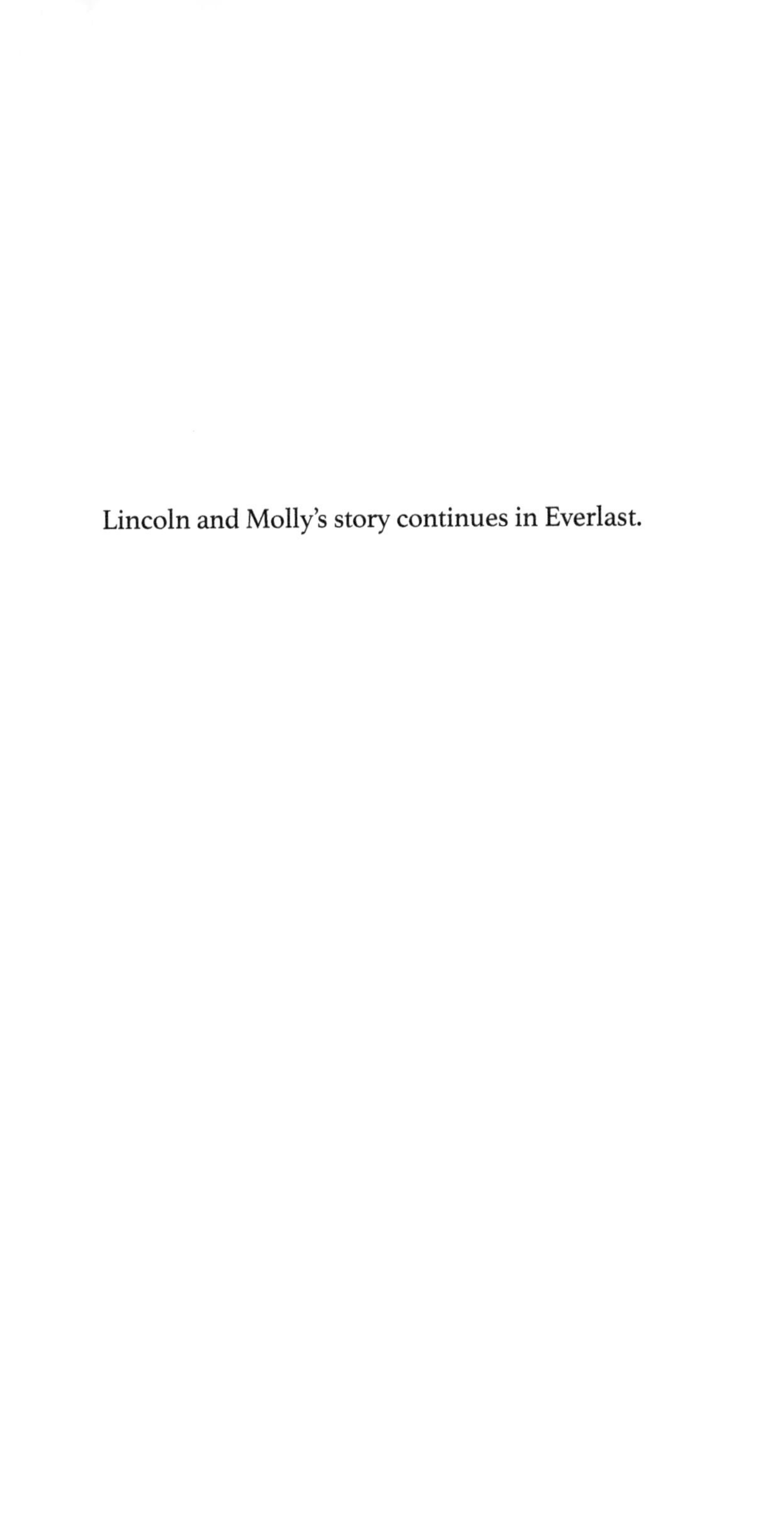

Lincoln and Molly's story continues in Everlast.

ALSO BY ALEX GRAYSON

THE JADED SERIES

Shatter Me

Reclaim Me

Unveil Me

Awaken Me

The Jaded Series: The Complete Collection

THE CONSUMED SERIES

Sex Junkie

Shamelessly Bare

Hungry Eyes

The Consumed Series: The Complete Collection

THE HELL NIGHT SERIES

Trouble in Hell

Bitter Sweet Hell

Judge of Hell

Key to Hell

The Hell Night Series: Complete Collection

STANDALONES

Endless Obsession

Whispered Prayers of a Girl

Pitch Dark

The Sinister Silhouette

Treacherous

Malicious

Lead Player

Forevermore

Everlast

ABOUT THE AUTHOR

Alex Grayson is a USA Today bestselling author of heart pounding, emotionally gripping contemporary romances including the Jaded Series, the Consumed Series, The Hell Night Series, and several standalone novels. Her passion for books was reignited by a gift from her sister-in-law. After spending several years as a devoted reader and blogger, Alex decided to write and independently publish her first novel in 2014 (an endeavor that took a little longer than expected). The rest, as they say, is history.

Originally a southern girl, Alex now lives in Ohio with her husband, two children, two cats and dog. She loves the color blue, homemade lasagna, casually browsing real estate, and interacting with her readers. Visit her website, www.alexgraysonbooks.com, or find her on social media!

Sign up for Alex's newsletter HERE!

Facebook
BookBub
Twitter

Instagram
Pinterest
Newsletter
Email

www.ingramcontent.com/pod-product-compliance
Lightning Source LLC
Chambersburg PA
CBHW070539310726
48982CB00010B/1406/J

* 9 7 8 1 7 3 5 1 9 8 2 4 8 *